P9-DXI-564

PEANUTS®

Peppermint Patty Goes to Camp!

by Charles M. Schulz
adapted by Maggie Testa
illustrated by Vicki Scott

Ready-to-Read

Simon Spotlight
New York London Toronto Sydney New Delhi

SIMON SPOTLIGHT
An imprint of Simon & Schuster Children's Publishing Division
1230 Avenue of the Americas, New York, New York 10020
This Simon Spotlight edition May 2016

For information about special discounts for bulk purchases, please contact Simon & Schuster Special Sales at 1-866-506-1949 or business@simonandschuster.com.
Manufactured in the United States of America 0316 LAK
2 4 6 8 10 9 7 5 3 1
ISBN 978-1-4814-6263-1 (hc)
ISBN 978-1-4814-6262-4 (pbk)
ISBN 978-1-4814-6264-8 (eBook)

Peppermint Patty sits up straight
at her desk and grips her pencil.
Her eyes are focused on the board.
But something isn't quite right
at school today, she realizes.
"Where is everyone?"
she asks.

"Oh right!" she shouts.
"Yesterday was the
last day of school.
School's out for summer!"
For Peppermint Patty
summer means one thing
and one thing only . . . camp!

Soon Peppermint Patty
is on the bus to Camp Remote!
She finds a seat next to Marcie.
They met at camp one year and
have been best friends ever since!
“I can’t wait to get there,”
Peppermint Patty says to Marcie.
“There are so many things to do!”

Peppermint Patty
loves swimming
by the lake,

sleeping in a cabin,

and singing songs
by the campfire.

She even likes eating
“camp chow.”
“Aren’t you going to eat, Marcie?”
she asks on their first night
of camp.
Marcie shakes her head.

Marcie doesn’t like camp
the way Peppermint Patty does.
“I always get lonely,”
she tells Peppermint Patty.
“But at least I can catch up
on my reading.”

"Can you imagine our teacher
expecting us to read four whole
books this summer?"
asks Peppermint Patty.
"I already read them all,"
says Marcie.
Peppermint Patty shakes
her head.

A few days later Peppermint Patty
sees something interesting.
Could it really be him?
Yes, it's Charlie Brown
at the boys' camp.
Peppermint Patty waves.
"Hi, Chuck!" she calls.

“He didn’t wave back, sir,”
Marcie points out.
“Stop calling me ‘sir’!”
says Peppermint Patty.
“Anyway, that must be because
he can’t see me. Let’s go.”

Peppermint Patty and Marcie walk around the lake.
Soon they are at the boys' camp.
"Hi, Chuck!" says Peppermint Patty.
"What are you doing here?" asks Charlie Brown.

“The girls’ camp is going to play the boys’ camp in a ball game,” Peppermint Patty explains. “Aren’t you going to play?”

“I don’t think I’m good enough,” says Charlie Brown.

"But you love baseball,"
says Peppermint Patty.
"This is summer camp.
You're here to have fun . . ."
Charlie Brown nods.
"No matter how lousy you are!"
Peppermint Patty adds.

The girls' camp
beat the boys' camp!

After the baseball game,
Peppermint Patty
looks for Charlie Brown.
“Great game, wasn’t it?” she asks.
“Sorry I had to strike you out.”

Back at the girls' camp,
Peppermint Patty decides to send
a letter to a very special someone.
"Dear, Chuck," she writes.
"Life here at camp is great."
Little does she know that Marcie
is also writing a letter to the
same special someone.

The next day Marcie receives
a reply from Charlie Brown,
but Peppermint Patty does not.
Suddenly, camp isn't as much
fun anymore!

Peppermint Patty marches over
to the boys' camp.
She wants to have a word
with Charlie Brown.
But he is nowhere to be found!
"He got lonely for Snoopy
so he went home," Linus explains.

Peppermint Patty is sad.
“I wonder if it’s because I struck
him out,” she says and sits down.
Linus holds out his blanket.
“Hold this for a while.
It’ll make you feel better,”
he promises.

Linus's blanket works!
Peppermint Patty is surprised
by how soft and cozy it is.
She feels much better already.
"If Snoopy were here,
he'd lean over and kiss me
on the cheek," she says.

"Like this?" asks Linus.
Then he leans over and
kisses her on the cheek!

Just at that moment,
Marcie comes over.
"Sir, the bus for home is leaving
in an hour," she says.
"Linus just kissed me on the cheek
and you tell me the bus is leaving?"
Peppermint Patty shouts.

“Never take a summer romance seriously, sir,” Marcie replies. “Stop calling me ‘sir’!” says Peppermint Patty.

On the bus ride home,
Peppermint Patty asks Marcie
a very important question.
“Why do you always call me ‘sir’
when I keep asking you not to?
Don’t you realize how annoying
that can be?”

“No, ma’am!” replies Marcie.

"So what are you going to do next summer, sir?" asks Marcie.
Peppermint Patty smiles.
She knows exactly what she'll do.

After all, for Peppermint Patty,
summer means one thing
and one thing only . . .
summer camp!